LET IT GLOW

Based on an original story by Suzanne Francis
Illustrated by the Disney Storybook Art Team

A GOLDEN BOOK • NEW YORK

Copyright © 2017 Disney Enterprises, Inc. All rights reserved. Published in the United States by Golden Books,
an imprint of Random House Children's Books, a division of Penguin Random House LLC, 1745 Broadway, New York, NY 10019,
and in Canada by Penguin Random House Canada Limited, Toronto. Golden Books, A Golden Book, A Big Golden Book, the G colophon,
and the distinctive gold spine are registered trademarks of Penguin Random House LLC.
randomhousekids.com
ISBN 978-0-7364-3678-6
Printed in the United States of America
10 9 8 7 6 5 4 3 2 1

Kristoff was excited. He was taking his friends to Troll Valley for the annual crystal ceremony!

"Grand Pabbie honors all the young trolls who have earned their level-one crystals," he explained. "It's a huge achievement."

Anna, Elsa, and Olaf couldn't wait to experience the mysterious tradition.

Bulda, the troll who had raised Kristoff, and a young troll named Little Rock greeted Kristoff and his friends when they arrived in Troll Valley. Little Rock was going to be in this year's ceremony.

Bulda explained that the ceremony had to be performed during autumn under the Northern Lights. But the Northern Lights were nowhere to be seen.

"And we only have a few more days before the last night of autumn," she added.

Anna noticed that Little Rock was holding four crystals in his hand. Three were glowing, but the fourth was dull.

"This is my tracking crystal," he explained. "It won't glow until I have excellent tracking skills. If I can't earn this last level-one crystal, I can't be in the ceremony."

"To be a good tracker, you need to be fearless, observant, and inventive," said Kristoff. "I know you can do it."

Just then, Little Rock noticed that Grand Pabbie was nowhere
in sight. Bulda thought he had gone to find a place where the
Northern Lights were visible.

"Why don't we track him?" suggested Kristoff. "Maybe you can
earn your crystal that way."

Little Rock smiled. "Yes!"

The trolls gave each of the friends a mossy cloak to keep warm.
Then Little Rock took the lead as they set out to find Grand Pabbie.

When the path split three ways, Little Rock stepped toward the first path.

"That goes back to Troll Valley," Kristoff told him.

Little Rock tried the second path.

"That's toward Arendelle," said Anna.

Little Rock pointed to the third path. "This way!"

His tracking skills clearly needed some work.

Suddenly, Little Rock stopped. "I'm picking up a scent," he declared. "I think it's Grand Pabbie!" He dropped to the ground and began sniffing along a trail . . . but it led straight to Sven's hoof.

Little Rock tried to cover his mistake. "Sven! Stop standing on Grand Pabbie's footprints!"

The group continued and soon reached a frozen river.

"Be careful," said Kristoff. "I don't know how solid the ice is."

"Don't worry," said Little Rock. "I already earned my ice-trekking crystal. This is definitely thick enough—" *Crack!*

The ice split beneath Little Rock's feet! Anna and Kristoff
grabbed him before he fell through.

"Elsa, can you help us get across?" asked Anna. The group
watched as Elsa sent swirls of ice into the air. The swirls
formed a stairway that arched over the river.

The group ran up the steps—then heard
a rumble when they started down the other
side. The riverbank beneath Elsa's stairway was
beginning to break off from the extra weight!

Elsa waved her arms, and some ice sleds appeared.
"Jump on!" she shouted. Everyone swooshed over the steps
and down the frozen river.

"You were both so fearless," Little Rock said to Anna and Elsa when they reached the other side. He handed the sisters a glowing crystal from his pouch. "You deserve to carry this."

It was getting light, so the group camped for the day and set out again the next night.

"We have to find Grand Pabbie right away," said Little Rock. "There are only two days of autumn left."

Little Rock picked up a branch, thinking it was a clue. "Grand Pabbie must have gone this way," he said.

"Arm!" cried Olaf. "I wondered where I'd left you."

Little Rock was disappointed.

"Everyone makes mistakes," said Kristoff. "And Olaf is lucky you were able to help him!"

Little Rock's mood brightened, and he quickly found another clue:
a clump of green moss. "It's from Grand Pabbie's cloak!" he exclaimed.
Elsa pointed out the thick patches of green scattered over the
ground. "It's possible that it's just moss," she said gently.
Little Rock sighed. "You're right. This isn't from Grand Pabbie's cloak."

Farther up the mountain, where the path was covered with snow, Anna discovered what seemed to be troll footprints. She called Little Rock over to take a look.

"These are Grand Pabbie's footprints!" he declared.

They followed the prints higher and higher up the mountain, but the marks stopped at the very top. Before the friends could investigate further, a snowstorm rolled in.

Little Rock offered to find shelter, but Elsa used
her magic to create a beautiful ice shelter instead.
The friends hurried inside.

After the storm had passed, the mountain was covered
with a fresh layer of snow, masking the footprints. The group
wanted to continue their search for Grand Pabbie.
"Maybe we could tumble down!" suggested Little Rock.

Olaf was the first to leap over the side of the mountain and start rolling. Little Rock curled into a ball and followed him, with Anna, Elsa, Kristoff, and Sven close behind.

The friends laughed as they slipped, slid, and rolled.

When they reached the bottom, Little Rock took out his snow crystal. "Olaf, you were observant when you found a way to get down the mountain. You deserve to carry this."

Olaf gasped. He was honored!

Little Rock continued to hunt for clues. He soon found a funny-looking bump under the snow. He dug in so deep that he disappeared—then popped out with a pickax and a rope in his hand.

"So *that's* where I left those!" said Kristoff. He had lost them the previous spring.

"I tracked some important stuff!" said Little Rock proudly.

"You *found* some important stuff," Kristoff corrected him.

The friends followed a trail that curved around the mountain and ended at the base of a giant waterfall. Anna found a mossy cloak there. It was Grand Pabbie's!

"He must have dropped it when he climbed the cliff," said Elsa.

They gazed up and wondered how they could reach the top of the cliff.

Sven stuck his tongue into the waterfall. Kristoff understood that the reindeer was suggesting that Elsa freeze the waterfall.

"What an inventive idea, Sven!" said Little Rock.

Elsa waved her arms, and the waterfall froze solid.
"Now we climb," said Kristoff. He handed Anna some
spikes for her shoes and his pickax. Then they began to
carefully scale the waterfall.

"I totally got this," said Anna as she struck the ice
with her tool and pulled herself up.

When Anna and Kristoff reached the top, they threw
the rope down and helped pull everyone else up.

"Kristoff and Sven," said Little Rock at the top of the waterfall, "because you were so inventive with the waterfall, you deserve to carry my water crystal."

He took a glowing crystal out of his pouch and handed it to Kristoff. Kristoff promised to keep it safe.

From the top of the falls, the group followed a trail as it climbed higher and higher. Soon the air became thick with fog. Little Rock grew nervous, but he kept going.

At the mountain peak, a figure appeared in the mist.

Little Rock ran and threw his arms around it. "Grand Pabbie!" he exclaimed.

Everyone watched in surprise as Little Rock hugged a troll-shaped boulder.

They couldn't believe he was still so bad at tracking!

Kristoff got Little Rock's attention and pointed to the real
Grand Pabbie, standing nearby. Confused, Little Rock looked at
the moss-covered rock he was hugging and then back at Grand
Pabbie.

"I tracked you!" he cried. He ran to the real Grand Pabbie and
gave him a giant hug.

"Hello, Little Rock," said the old troll.

Little Rock pulled out his tracking crystal and his face fell.
He was sure he had gained tracking skills, but it was still dull!

"I bet there's just something wrong with the crystal," said
Kristoff.

"No, that's not it," said Little Rock. "I'm not very good at
tracking. If anyone here has earned a tracking crystal, it's all
of you. I needed your help to get here."

"Look!" said Anna suddenly. Little Rock's tracking crystal was glowing!

"But I didn't earn it," said Little Rock.

"Actually, you did," said Grand Pabbie. "You figured out what it takes to be a good tracker." For Little Rock, that meant understanding that he needed help from his friends. The knowledge made the crystal glow!

Just then, the other level-one trolls came out of hiding.
"Hooray for Little Rock!" they cheered.

Grand Pabbie and the trolls had been waiting for Little Rock to find them and make his final crystal glow. It was time for the crystal ceremony to begin.

"Oh, I need my other crystals now," Little Rock said
shyly to his friends.

They smiled as they each handed over the crystals
he had given them to carry earlier.

With all his crystals glowing, Little Rock joined Grand Pabbie
and the other young trolls. They raised their crystals in the air,
and the Northern Lights reflected the colors and bounced them
back into the sky, where they glowed even brighter.
But they weren't as bright as Grand Pabbie had hoped.

Elsa had an idea. She waved her arms, and a giant magical snowflake appeared in the sky. It turned in a circle, sparkling and reflecting the Northern Lights into the sky all around them. The lights were very bright and beautiful.

"That is so much better!" said Grand Pabbie.

Back in Troll Valley, Bulda noticed the intense colors in the sky.
"Everybody look up!" she shouted. All the trolls knew immediately
what the bright lights meant: Little Rock had completed his quest!
Thanks to Little Rock and the other level-one trolls, the Northern
Lights were shining brightly again, and the rest of Troll Valley would
remember this night forever.

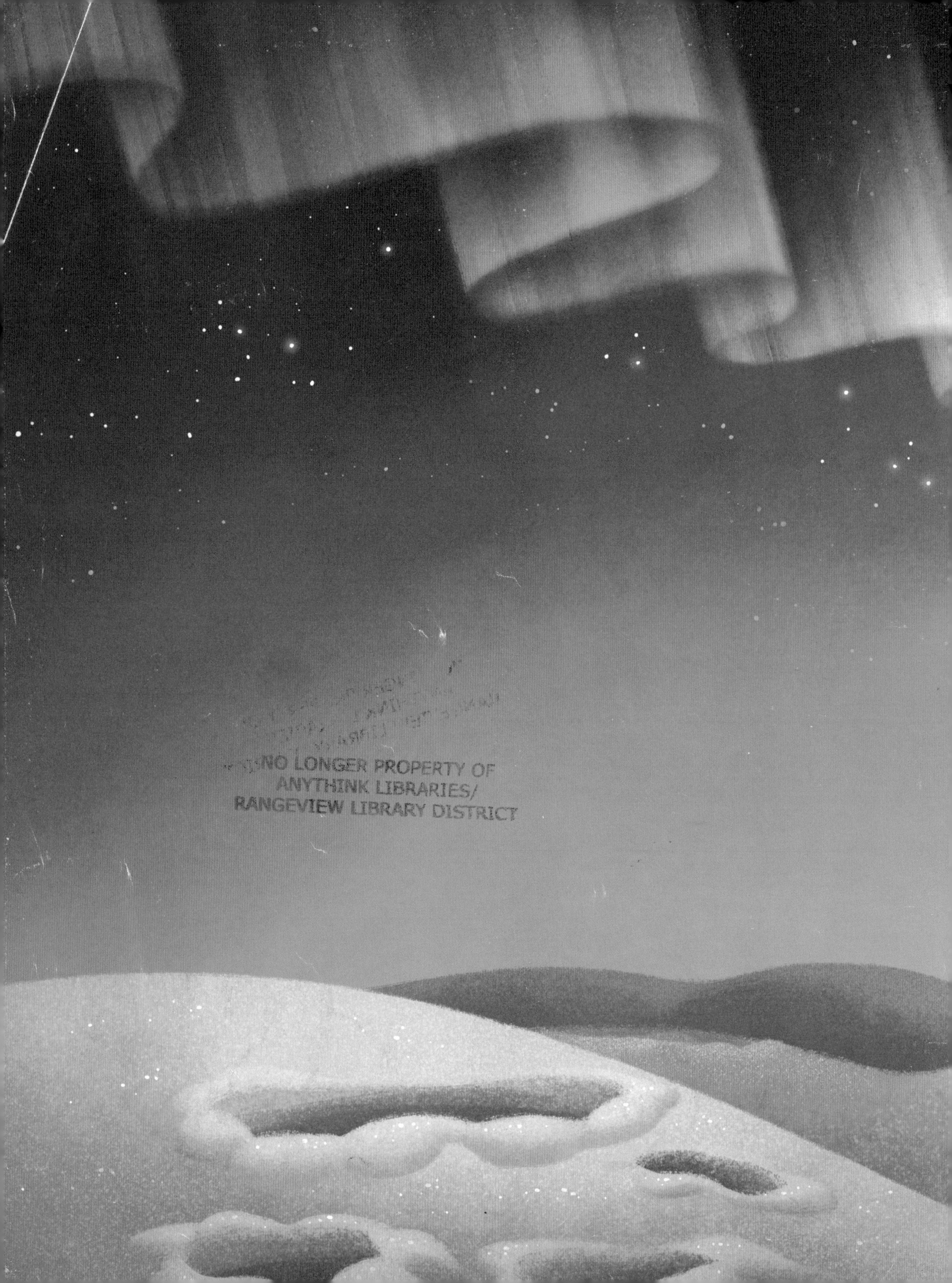